STAGE
5

BOOK 4

LIFT RIDDLE

John Townsend

Beth was over the moon. Brad was DJ-ing at a big party and Beth was going too. Brad said he'd film her singing so she could put it online.

"Then you'll dazzle the world," he said as they got to the lift. Beth was really keen. "Come on, Dad. We're late."

The lift doors slid open. Lee and JJ were on their way down.
"Hi, Beth," Lee said. "Good luck for your big night."

4

"You'll see me when I put the video online," Beth giggled.
Brad pressed the button to go down.

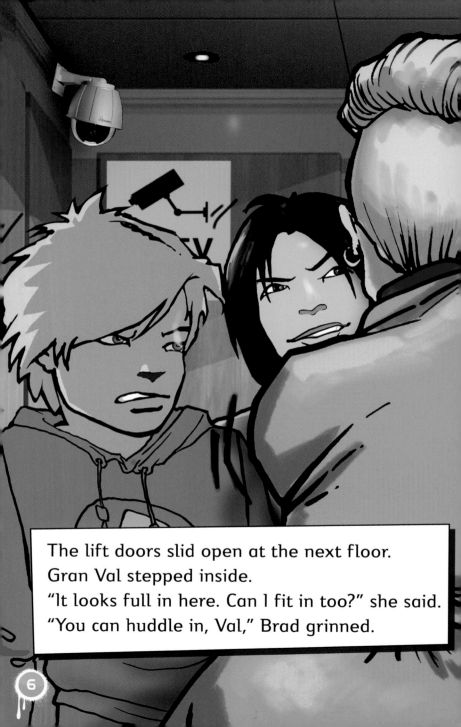

The lift doors slid open at the next floor.
Gran Val stepped inside.
"It looks full in here. Can I fit in too?" she said.
"You can huddle in, Val," Brad grinned.

The doors slid shut just as Gran Val laughed, "Ooh, how silly of me. I'm in a muddle." She pressed the button again. "I need to get out. I forgot my bag."

But the doors didn't open and the lift didn't move. "Press it again," Brad said. Nothing happened.

It's no good. It's jammed.

Brad shook his head.

But we'll miss the party.

Beth gave a little sigh.

11

Gran Val said, "I hate small spaces. I get in a frazzle and I was already in a muddle." "Keep calm, Val," Brad smiled. "We'll cheer you up with a song."

Brad turned on his disco
bubble machine and Beth sang.

13

14

Gran Val was in a panic again.
"Don't fiddle with it. We might crash!"

Lee tried not to giggle. "Don't worry,
Gran Val. We'll be fine."

"I felt something wobble," Val gulped.
"I think we're moving," JJ said.
"It feels like we're going up," Lee cheered.

The doors slid open at last.
"We're home," Brad said.
"You can all come in and
chill. I'll put the kettle on."

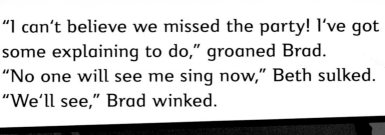

"I can't believe we missed the party! I've got some explaining to do," groaned Brad.
"No one will see me sing now," Beth sulked.
"We'll see," Brad winked.

You too

Sear

1:45 / 1:45

＋ Add to ▼   Share ⚑

360p

786,209

2,284 likes, 6,472 dislikes

As Seen On:
Just Jared

Show more ≫

Beth's singing dazzled the world after all, and soon they were all famous!